The
Long Journey
to
Freedom

by
Susan Grohmann

Perfection Learning®

Illustration: Margo Bock
Design: Tobi Cunningham

About the Author

Born in Massachusetts, Susan Grohmann has also lived in Maryland and studied in New York City. A resident of southern Florida since 1970, she usually mistakes herself for a native Floridian.

Ms. Grohmann's interest in writing dates back to the seventh grade. Reading to her two sons, now in their teens, inspired her to begin creating children's stories for publication.

During the past several years, Ms. Grohmann has enjoyed volunteering in public classrooms, helping third and fourth graders improve their writing skills. When it comes to relaxation, she enjoys crossword puzzles.

© 2002 Perfection Learning®
www.perfectionlearning.com

6 7 8 9 10 11 QG 17 16 15 14 13 12
QG/Dubuque, Iowa
5/12

38565
PB ISBN: 978-0-7891-5616-7
RLB ISBN: 978-0-7569-0451-7

Printed in the United States of America

Contents

Foreword

This story is set in Florida during the First Seminole War. The historical details are accurate. The following historical characters really did exist: Chief Billy Bowlegs, Nero, Abraham, General Andrew Jackson, and Alexander Arbuthnot. Most of the places in the story do or did exist.

However, the Miller Plantation and the characters living there are fictional, as are most of the characters living in Bowlegs Town and Nero's Town.

In 1818, Nero's Town was the largest maroon community in the South. A *maroon community* was made up of former slaves who had escaped or been set free.

FLORIDA TERRITORY
1818

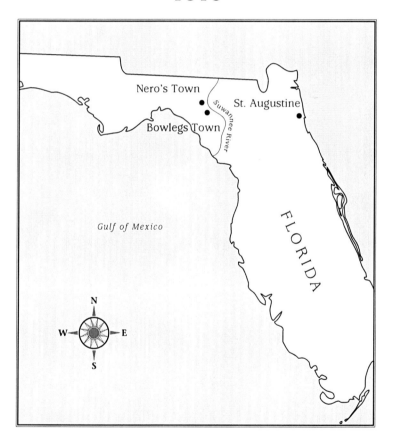

Nero's Town

St. Augustine

Bowlegs Town

Suwannee River

Gulf of Mexico

FLORIDA

N
W E
S

1

The Book

"My mother ran like the wind," Catbird said. "But the people chasing her were catching up. Then she picked up speed and—"

Suddenly Kwaku's tall form filled the doorway of the cabin.

"Tilly," he said, "it's time to carry the eggs to the big house."

"Please, Father, just one more minute," Tilly begged. "Mother hasn't finished the story."

"You've heard that story many times," Kwaku reminded his daughter. "You know how it ends. Your grandmother outran the other players and scored. Her team won the big ball game."

"Oh, Father," Tilly sighed, "now you've spoiled it."

The story seemed new to Tilly every time. She never grew tired of hearing about her mother's girlhood in Georgia. Some of the stories were exciting. Others were sad.

The saddest story was Catbird's kidnapping. She'd been asleep in her Yuchi Indian village. Her father was away hunting deer in the forest. Men from a rival tribe had entered the village on horseback. They dragged 12-year-old Catbird from her bed. She was carried off and sold. Torn from her family, Catbird had become a slave of white people.

"The eggs, Tilly," Kwaku reminded his daughter.

"It's not fair," Tilly complained. "It's Sunday. No one else has to work."

"Just one small chore," Catbird said. "When you get back from the big house, I'll tell you another story."

"And remember to count your blessings," Tilly's father added. "You're already 11 years old. In a year, you would have been sent out to the fields. You're lucky that your mother taught you to sew. You'll get to stay here every day and make clothes. Would you rather plant rice in the hot sun?"

Tilly hung her head. "No, sir."

As a girl, Tilly's mother had learned to stitch beads on strips of leather. Yuchi women wore the beaded bands in their hair. Catbird had also made clothes for her owners and the other slaves.

A slave who could sew didn't have to do fieldwork. This is why Catbird had taught Tilly to sew.

"So what are you going to do now?" Kwaku asked Tilly.

"Carry the eggs to the big house and not complain about it." Tilly looked up at her father.

"That's right." Kwaku's stern look changed into a wide grin. He was always handsome, but more so when he smiled. His white teeth glowed against the deep brown of his skin. Tilly could see why her mother had fallen for him.

Tilly often begged to hear the story of how her parents met. Catbird hadn't been a slave very long before she ran away. She'd planned to find her way back to her village. But Catbird's owner had hunted the young girl down.

Her owner decided she was working too near her former home. If she were farther away, she wouldn't dare try to escape.

So Catbird was sold to a different white man named Mr. Miller. Mr. Miller was British. He was on his way to northern Florida. There he would start a rice plantation. In the cart headed for Florida, Catbird wept bitterly.

Then the cart stopped at a port city. Mr. Miller bought some people who had just arrived on a ship. Many had not survived the sea voyage from West Africa. But Kwaku had survived. He was a strong young man of 16. Mr. Miller knew Kwaku would be a good worker.

As soon as she saw Kwaku, Catbird felt better. She and Kwaku looked at each other often during the long trip to Florida. Mr. Miller had filled the cart with supplies at the port. Then he made the slaves walk the rest of the way.

All this had happened many years ago. Now the year was 1815. Tilly's parents were still Mr. Miller's property. Because he owned her parents, Mr. Miller owned Tilly as well.

Mr. Miller's rice plantation had made him very rich. Kwaku and Catbird had helped to start the plantation in the wilderness. To thank them, Mr. Miller let them keep chickens. But they had to share the eggs with Mr. Miller's family.

Tilly carried a basket to the henhouse. She gently placed fresh eggs in the basket. As she worked, she thought about the way her parents had met.

Tilly had mixed feelings about the story. She was sad because her parents were separated from their families and had lost their freedom. Still, she was happy that Kwaku and Catbird had found each other. They'd been married on the Florida plantation.

Tilly walked up the path to the big house. She climbed the steps to the back porch and knocked on the kitchen door.

"Come in," called a young girl's voice. It was Lydia Miller, the plantation owner's daughter. Like Tilly, Lydia was 11.

Lydia was sitting in the kitchen drinking a glass of milk. A book lay open on the table in front of her. When Tilly delivered eggs, she often saw Lydia reading.

Lydia had on a ruffled dress of pale green silky fabric. Tilly hated her simple, tattered blue dress. Every slave wore "Negro cloth," a coarse blend of wool and cotton.

"Put the eggs on the counter," Lydia ordered. She didn't look up from her book.

Tilly carefully placed the eggs in a bowl. From where she stood, she could see over Lydia's shoulder. Tilly gazed at a picture of a girl in a flower garden. The girl had beautiful ringlets. She wore a pink dress with lace trim.

Tilly put the last egg into the bowl. She edged closer to the table. Now she could see that the girl in the picture looked sad. Tears glistened on her cheeks.

The girl in the book was wealthy and pretty like Lydia. Why was she crying? Tilly stared at the marks on the page across from the picture. She knew those words explained why the girl was unhappy. Tilly wished she could read them.

"I feel you staring," Lydia said suddenly. She turned in her chair and glared at Tilly. Her glossy, light brown ringlets bounced around her neck. "Don't you dare stand so close to me," she snapped.

Tilly backed away. "I—I'm sorry," she stammered. "I just wanted to see the picture."

Lydia slammed the book shut. "Well, you can't. Lowly zambo slaves are not allowed to look at books. You've done your errand. Now go."

Tilly's face burned with shame. She'd heard the word *zambo* before. The term described a person with one African parent and one Indian parent.

Kwaku always told Tilly she was beautiful. "You are a perfect blend of the best of two worlds," he would say. But Lydia spat out the word in a nasty tone. The way Lydia spoke made Tilly feel worthless.

"Lydia!" Tilly recognized the voice of Mrs. Miller, the mistress of the house.

Mrs. Miller had chosen Tilly's name. Her parents had never been asked if they liked it. Kwaku once said he would have given her an African name. He was proud of his own. It meant he had been born on a Wednesday.

"Coming, Mother," Lydia replied. She got up and left the room. The book lay on the table.

Tilly went outside. Halfway across the back porch, she stopped. Before she knew what her feet were doing, she was back in the kitchen. Her hands picked up the book and hid it under her dress.

On the path to her cabin, Tilly's brain scolded her. Are you crazy? What are you doing? Take the book back right now! You'll be in so much trouble. Your parents will be in trouble too.

Yet her legs kept carrying her back to the slave street. Other slaves greeted her as she went. Tilly said hello, keeping her arms crossed in front of her. She couldn't let them see the bulge under her dress.

Tilly finally arrived at her cabin. Her family shared the cabin with another family. A wall divided the building into two living spaces.

Tilly peered through the door of her family's room. It was empty.

Tilly could hear her parents' voices on the other side of the wall. They were visiting their elderly neighbors, Samantha and Samson.

Tilly's bed was a simple wood frame in a corner of the room. Her father had built it.

Because Kwaku was a fine carpenter, he never worked in the rice fields. Instead he built slave cabins, outbuildings, and furniture. Sometimes he made repairs on the big house. Once he had added several rooms to the mansion.

A mattress sewn from potato sacks covered Tilly's bed frame. The mattress was stuffed with pine needles. Her head spinning, Tilly shoved Lydia's book under the mattress. Shaking and breathless, Tilly sat down on the bed. She felt both thrilled and terrified by what she'd done.

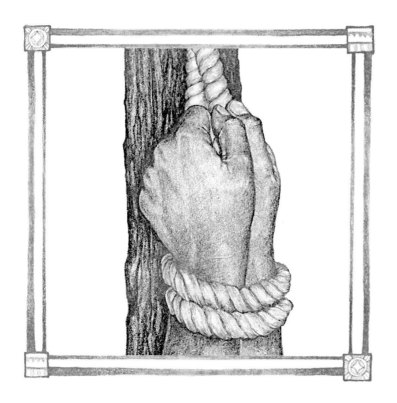

2

The Lash

For a long time, Tilly remained very still. All her excitement drained away. Only fear was left. She'd made a terrible mistake. How could she have been so foolish? She'd placed herself and her parents in danger. Maybe it wasn't too late to return the book.

Tilly got up and pulled the book out from under her mattress. She knew she must hurry back to the big house. Yet she stood for a while with the book in her hands. She felt sure a magical world lay between its covers. Tilly longed to visit that world. Just holding the book, she felt closer to her dream.

Tilly tucked the book beneath her dress. She started back toward the big house.

"There's the sneaky little thief," Lydia's voice cried out.

Tilly gasped. Her heart began to race. She'd waited too long. Lydia hurried toward Tilly. She was pulling her father along by the hand. Even worse, Mr. Stroud was with them.

Mr. Stroud was the plantation overseer. He made sure all the slaves did their jobs. If their work did not please him, he punished them. If they broke any plantation rules, he punished them. Mr. Stroud seemed to enjoy punishing the slaves with his whip.

"Slow down, Lydia," Mr. Miller panted.

The sound of the master's voice brought Kwaku and Catbird outdoors. Samantha and Samson also stepped outside. They were like a grandmother and grandfather to Tilly. She didn't know her own grandparents.

"She has the book under her dress!" Lydia shouted. "I can see it."

"Tilly, what are you hiding under your dress?" Mr. Miller asked.

Slowly, Tilly drew out the book and held it toward Lydia. Lydia snatched it.

"I was right, Father," she said. "I told you she stole it."

Tilly began to tremble. Her parents came and stood beside her. Kwaku put his arm around her shoulder.

"What's this about, Tilly?" he asked.

"I—I was bringing it back," Tilly stuttered. "I j—just wanted to hold it for a m—minute. I'm s—sorry."

"That's two rules she broke," Mr. Stroud said. "She's not allowed to have a book. And she stole from Miss Lydia. What should be done with such a wicked child, Mr. Miller?"

Tilly stood frozen in fear.

"Miss Lydia has her book back," Kwaku said. "And my daughter has said she's sorry. She knows she's done wrong."

"Oh, she acts sorry now," Mr. Stroud answered. "But just wait until we leave. They'll all laugh about the trick she played on Miss Lydia."

"Our daughter did something bad," Catbird said. "We would never joke about that."

By now all the other slaves had come out of their cabins. Everyone stared at Mr. Miller. What would he decide?

Lydia looked up at her father with pitiful eyes. "It's my favorite book, Father. I was so afraid she'd ruin it. Now my whole day is spoiled."

"Bring Tilly to the whipping post," Mr. Miller ordered finally. "She'll receive ten lashes."

Mr. Miller looked up and down the slave street. "All of you must watch her be punished. No one can steal from my home and get away with it."

Tilly's knees wobbled. Spots swam before her eyes. Mr. Stroud grabbed her by the arm.

"No need for that," Kwaku said. "I'll bring her." He put his hands on Tilly's shoulders and pushed her forward. Tilly walked in a panicked daze with her father.

"Please don't let him beat me, Father," Tilly whispered.

"You acted foolishly," he said. "Now you must take your punishment."

The whipping post stood at the end of the slave street. Mr. Stroud always left his cat-o'-nine-tails hanging from the post. He wanted the slaves to see it every day.

The cat-o'-nine-tails had a wooden handle covered in leather. Nine long leather straps were fixed to the handle. A knot had been tied at the end of each strap.

"Do I have to stay, Father?" Lydia asked, her face

pale. She had wanted to get Tilly in trouble. But she'd never thought about Tilly being whipped as punishment.

"Of course not, my dear," her father told her. "Take your book back to the house."

Tilly's dress was yanked off her shoulders. Her hands were tied to a ring at the top of the post. Mr. Stroud whipped the lash once in the air. The straps whistled near Tilly's ear.

Tilly began to scream. "No! No! Father! Father, help me!"

The whip struck her back. Her skin burned. Tilly heard herself yelp. The world began to spin before her eyes. She heard the crack of the leather straps a second time. But the straps did not touch her.

"Get out of the way!" Mr. Stroud shouted.

Tilly turned her head as far as she could. Kwaku had stepped between Tilly and Mr. Stroud. The cat-o'-nine-tails had struck Tilly's father.

"I told you to move!" Mr. Stroud roared. But Kwaku stayed put.

Mr. Stroud pushed Kwaku. He fell to his knees. Mr. Stroud raised the cat-o'-nine-tails above his head. Kwaku jumped up. Again he stood between his child and the whip.

Mr. Stroud turned to Mr. Miller, waiting to be told what to do.

"He wants to take the beating for his daughter. Let him do so," Mr. Miller said. "But give him twice as many lashes. Then lock him in the cell for five days."

The cell was a tiny brick room with a heavy wooden door. A single window let in light and air. But the window was too high for a prisoner to see out.

In the cell, Kwaku would be chained to the wall. No other slave would be allowed to speak to him. He would get one cup of water and one crust of bread each day.

Tilly's hands were untied. She rushed to her mother. Catbird gently pulled Tilly's dress back up onto her shoulders.

Tilly clung to her mother's neck. She could hear the whip dig into her father's back again and again. She squeezed her eyes shut.

Kwaku didn't make a sound.

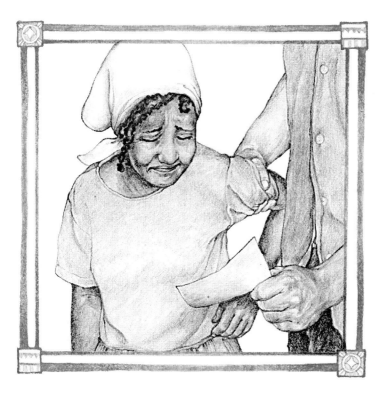

3

Terrible News

"It's all my fault," Tilly moaned. Her tears soaked Samantha's lap.

"Don't be so hard on yourself." Samantha's wrinkled hand smoothed Tilly's hair. "Master Miller and Mr. Stroud are to blame. You did a foolish thing. But you shouldn't be beaten for making a mistake."

"What if Father dies?" Tilly asked.

"Nonsense," Samantha said. "He won't die. He's much too strong in body and will. He's going to be just fine."

"What if he never forgives me?"

"He's forgiven you already," Samantha told her. "Hush now and go to sleep. It's very late. You're keeping your mother awake. Tomorrow she must get up early to sew and do laundry."

Samantha began to hum softly. The next thing Tilly knew, the big bell was clanging. Six days a week the bell called the slaves to work at sunrise.

Catbird had built a blaze in the fireplace. Now she stirred cornmeal and water in a pot over the fire.

Tilly sat up in bed.

"Does your back hurt?" Catbird asked.

"Not too much," Tilly said.

"Then get dressed and eat," Catbird told her. "Don't be late with the eggs."

"I don't want to go to the big house," Tilly argued.

"But you must," her mother replied. "Life doesn't stop because you made a mistake. We all have to go on doing our jobs."

After breakfast, Tilly walked very slowly with the basket of eggs. She stood outside the kitchen door, afraid to knock.

The door swung open, almost knocking Tilly down. The cook carried out a pan of dirty dishwater. She emptied the pan over the porch rail.

"Why are you lurking out here?" she asked sharply.

Tilly looked down at her feet.

"It's safe to come in." The cook's voice softened. "No one's in the kitchen but me."

The cook was a slave too. But as a house slave, her life was easier than that of a field slave. Still, her life was not her own.

Tilly quickly put the eggs in the bowl on the counter. As she left the kitchen, Tilly heard footsteps behind her. She didn't turn around. She just walked faster.

"Tilly, wait," called Lydia.

Tilly stopped and turned. Lydia held out the book to her.

"I feel bad," Lydia said. "I'm sorry your father's in the cell. You can have the book."

Tilly shook her head. She didn't want to touch the book. She hated that book with her whole being.

"Go ahead," Lydia said. "Take it. Don't be afraid. This time no one will know."

Again Tilly shook her head.

"I never should have tried to be nice to you!" Lydia snapped. She flounced back to the house.

Tilly didn't go straight home. She crept among some bushes near the cell. From her hiding place, she looked around. Mr. Stroud was nowhere in sight.

Tilly hurried to the cell. She pressed her cheek against the boards of the big door. "I'm so sorry, Father," she whispered. "Please don't hate me."

No sound came from inside. With all her soul, Tilly wanted to call out to her father. Then she thought about what would happen if she were caught. Her family's troubles would multiply. Gathering up her skirt, Tilly ran to her cabin.

The rest of the day dragged by. Tilly missed her father more with each passing hour. She worried about him every minute. Would his back heal? Would he starve?

Each day, Tilly helped the other children carry water to the fields. The workers labored long hours under the sun. They needed something to drink. Tilly usually sang and laughed with the other children. Now she didn't feel playful. She carried her bucket in silence.

The next day, Tilly went to the cell again. Going there was risky. But she couldn't stay away.

She watched from the bushes for a while. Seeing no one, Tilly walked to the cell door and raised her fist to knock. Then she shoved her hand into her pocket. Don't make things worse, she warned herself.

She started to leave. But before she knew it, she was back at the door. She had to hear her father's voice just once. Tilly tapped on the door.

"Father?" she called.

"Aha! I knew I'd catch you!" Mr. Stroud stepped around the corner.

Tilly screamed and turned to run. Mr. Stroud grabbed her.

"Tilly?" Kwaku called from inside the cell.

"Yes," Mr. Stroud called back. "I have your Tilly. I thought I saw her running from here the other day. I knew she'd be back. So I waited. Can't stop breaking rules, can she?"

Tilly squirmed in his grip. His fingers dug into her arm.

"She's proud like her father," Mr. Stroud said. He spoke loudly enough for Kwaku to hear. "Her father tried to make a fool of me. But he won't defy me again."

With his free hand, Mr. Stroud took a piece of paper out of his pocket. "Do you know what this paper says?"

Mr. Stroud waved the paper in Tilly's face. "This paper says your father will be sold. He'll go to another plantation, far away. But you and your mother will stay here."

Tilly's heart seemed to stop beating. She stared at the marks on the paper. Did the words really say that? If only she knew.

"We'll just see how proud your father is then," Mr. Stroud said. He let go of Tilly's arm. "Get out of here," he ordered.

Tilly ran blindly to the slave street. Near her cabin she collided with Samson.

"Whoa there, Tilly," he said. "Why the rush?"

"Oh, Samson!" Tilly cried. "It's so awful."

"What is it?" Samson guided her into his side of the cabin. Tilly dropped onto the bed. Samson eased down beside her. "What's so awful?"

Tilly couldn't answer right away. She could only cry. At last, she told him what Mr. Stroud had said.

"And I'm to blame," she wept. "I have to make things right. What can I do?"

Samson stayed silent until Tilly looked up at him. Then he shook his head sadly.

"Master Miller owns us," Samson said. "He decides our fate. We can't do anything about it."

Three more long days passed. Tilly was filled with dread. She wanted her father to be let out of the cell. But when he was, her family would be split up.

At the end of the fifth day, Mr. Stroud unlocked the cell door. He went inside to unfasten the chains.

Tilly and Catbird were waiting down the path for

Kwaku. He came toward them, head held high. Tilly loved to watch her father walk. He moved with grace. He held his back straight and his shoulders square. Kwaku never seemed to hurry. Yet he was always a few steps ahead of everyone else.

Tilly ran to him and flung her arms around his waist. "I'm sorry," she whispered. "It's my fault Master Miller is going to sell you."

"Don't worry, Tilly," Kwaku told her.

"Mother doesn't know," Tilly added. "I couldn't bear to tell her."

"Good," Kwaku said. "She doesn't need to know. I'll take care of things."

Two days passed. On the second night, the family huddled in the dark in their cabin. Kwaku had asked Samantha and Samson to be there. He spoke in a whisper.

"Tomorrow we will leave this plantation forever," he said.

"How?" Catbird asked. "If we run through the woods, the master's dogs will sniff us out."

"A wagon leaves here tomorrow for St. Augustine," Kwaku explained. "It will be carrying goods for sale in the city. Lucas will be driving the horses."

Lucas was a slave trusted by Master Miller. The master sent Lucas on errands far from the plantation. Lucas could be counted on to return.

"I've spoken to Lucas," Kwaku went on. "We'll leave before sunrise and wait by the road. Lucas will stop for us. We'll ride with him to St. Augustine."

"What will you do there?" Samantha asked.

"The Spaniards who rule Florida govern from St. Augustine," Kwaku explained. "I was told that they have freed many slaves. A slave who joins the Spanish church is set free immediately. There are other ways to gain freedom in St. Augustine. I'll go before the court there and plead our case."

"What if the court won't listen?" Samantha asked.

"In St. Augustine, every slave gets a day in court," Kwaku replied. "The court frees slaves from cruel masters. So I'll tell the court about the cell. The court will hear how Tilly was going to be whipped."

"We'll pray that the court grants you freedom," Samson said. "But we'll miss the three of you."

"You must come along," Kwaku told him.

Samson and Samantha looked at each other. Two gray heads shook from side to side.

"We are much too old," Samantha said.

"That's why you must escape now," Kwaku replied. "When you can no longer work, the master might stop feeding you."

"I don't think the master would ever do that," Samantha said.

"We were both born into slavery," Samson added. "We wouldn't know what to do with freedom."

"I hope you'll change your minds before morning," Kwaku said.

4

A Plan Gone Wrong

Samantha and Samson hugged Tilly and her family and wished them well. Tilly's heart ached. Samantha and Samson had decided to stay on the plantation.

The dark sky was still sprinkled with stars. The family walked softly out to the main road. Kwaku carried his tools. Tilly carried a bundle of extra clothes. Catbird carried some food.

Without speaking, they hurried along the road. Soon they could no longer see the big house.

"We could wait there," Catbird said. She pointed to a thicket of bushes alongside the road.

Behind a screen of branches, Tilly rested silently. Her heavy eyelids drooped. Someone began to shake her.

"Wake up, Tilly," her mother said. "The wagon is coming. Don't forget your bundle."

Pale dawn light had erased the stars. Tilly followed her parents to the edge of the road. The rumble of hooves and wooden wheels drew closer.

"Why isn't Lucas slowing down?" Catbird asked.

Tilly stared at the person holding the reins. "That isn't Lucas!" she cried. "Someone else is driving!"

The wagon shot past them. In dismay, they watched it vanish around a bend. The wheels sent up a cloud of dust. The three stood in shocked silence as the dust settled on them.

"Kwaku, what will we do?" Catbird asked after a moment.

"We'll start walking," Kwaku answered.

"Yes," Catbird said. "We should head back before we're missed."

"We won't go back to the plantation," Kwaku stated. He began walking in the direction the wagon had gone. "We'll head for St. Augustine."

Catbird and Tilly followed him.

"How far is it?" Tilly asked.

"Don't think about that," Kwaku told her. "One step at a time will get us there."

"We don't have much food," Catbird reminded him.

"We won't go back," Kwaku repeated.

Tilly watched the sun climb higher and higher. The air around them grew steamy. She felt as if they had been walking for a whole day.

"It's so hot," Tilly said. "I'm thirsty."

"I see a hammock up ahead," Kwaku told her. "When we get there, you can rest in the shade. I'll look for a creek."

Just as they reached the hammock, Tilly heard a far-off sound. The sound grew louder.

"I hear a wagon," Tilly said. "It's coming from St. Augustine."

"Maybe the master's wagon is coming back for us," Catbird said.

"I don't think so," Kwaku said. "We'd better hide in the hammock."

They slipped in among the trees. The wagon drove up to the hammock and stopped. Tilly and her parents ducked behind some palmettos.

Six men got out of the wagon. They began fixing one of the wheels.

Three of the men were black. Two were Indian. Tilly couldn't decide about the sixth man. Was he Indian or black? Perhaps, Tilly thought, he's a mixture like me.

The men wore knee-length shirts with collars and long, full sleeves. The shirts were gathered at the waist by colorful belts. Each man wore several scarves tied around his neck.

The wheel repair seemed to take forever. Tilly didn't think she could stay still much longer. At last the job was done. The men began climbing back into the wagon.

Just then, something brushed past Tilly's foot. She looked down and saw a rattlesnake slither by. Tilly screamed and jumped up.

Her sudden movement frightened the rattler. It streaked away into the bushes. The six men spun around. They grabbed rifles from the wagon.

"Come out of there," one of the men ordered.

"Stand where we can see you," said another.

Rifle barrels pointed at the family as they stepped into the open. Tilly cowered behind her father.

"We're headed for St. Augustine," Kwaku explained.

The men lowered their guns.

"Where are you from?" one of them asked. "Are you runaways?"

"Please let us go on our way," Catbird begged.

"Get in the wagon," the man said.

"These men are armed," Kwaku said quietly. "We must do as we are told."

When everyone was aboard, the wagon rumbled on down the road. They were headed away from St. Augustine and their chance for freedom.

In the back of the wagon, Catbird shivered in fear. Tilly had never seen her mother look so frightened. Catbird began to wail in the Yuchi tongue. She looked toward the sky as if she were praying for help.

One of the Indian men turned and spoke to Catbird in Yuchi. She gazed at the man.

"What did he say, Mother?" Tilly asked.

"He said that The Master of Breath has not forgotten us."

Tilly knew that the Yuchi people called their main god *The Master of Breath*.

"He said not to be afraid," Catbird went on. "He told me our lives will be better from now on."

Still, Tilly trembled inside. She wished she could go back to the plantation. She longed for her familiar cabin. She wanted to see Samantha and Samson.

The wagon rolled on and on. The sun dropped

lower in the sky. At last it shone straight into Tilly's eyes. Then the wagon entered a town of wooden houses. Fields of corn waved in the breeze nearby.

Indian men, women, and children gathered around the wagon. The women had on short blouses and long skirts. Many loops of bright beads circled each woman's neck.

Everyone seemed to be talking at once. The two Indians got down from the wagon. They went inside one of the houses.

An Indian girl brought water for Tilly and her parents. Tilly gulped the water eagerly.

Before long, the two Indian men came out of the house. They returned to the wagon. The man who spoke Yuchi talked to Catbird. When he finished speaking, Catbird covered her face with her hands.

"What did he say?" Kwaku asked his wife.

Catbird couldn't seem to answer. She could only shake her head. Kwaku rubbed her back, trying to soothe her.

The wagon driver snapped the reins. The wagon began to move again. The three black men were still in the wagon. The man who was part black and part Indian was driving.

Tilly had gone weak all over with fear. Something dreadful must be about to happen to them. She had to know what it was.

"Please, Mother," Tilly begged, "tell us what's going on."

Catbird lifted her head. She took a deep breath.

"The Yuchi man told me that his chief owns these men," she said. "We're being taken to the place where they live."

Tilly couldn't believe her ears. Looking at her father, she saw horror in his eyes.

Had they escaped from the plantation only to become slaves somewhere else?

5

A New Life

A crowd of men and women raced around the big field. Wild shouts filled the air. Catbird's shouts were the loudest of all.

A small deerskin ball was tossed in a high arc. Tiger ran toward the ball. In each hand, he carried a long stick. A small net was fastened to the end of each stick. Tiger caught the ball between the two nets. He hurled the ball out of the nets to a player on his team.

The ball was passed from one pair of nets to another. Soon a great cheer rose. Tiger's team had won the ball game.

Tilly and Catbird joined in the cheering. They knew Kwaku had placed bets on Tiger's team. Everyone in Bowlegs Town gambled on the ball games. Kwaku might have blankets or a new ax to bring home.

"Let's go see what your father won," Catbird said.

"Why don't you ever join the games?" Tilly asked as they walked.

"I'm too old now," Catbird said. She was smiling. "But it's so good to be able to watch again," she added.

"Life has been so much better for us this past year," Tilly said. "Tiger told you it would be." Tiger was the man who had spoken Yuchi in the wagon.

"I'm less homesick for my village now," Catbird agreed. "At Bowlegs Town, I can speak my own language. I can take part in the festivals I remember from childhood."

When they found Kwaku, he showed them a shiny cooking pot that he'd won.

Tiger walked over and put his arm around Kwaku's

shoulder. "You're a smart man," he said. "You know a winning team when you see one."

Tiger was the son of Yuchi Indians. He'd come with them to Florida when he was a small boy.

All Indians living in Florida were known as Seminoles. They had moved from places north of Florida. They came from many tribes and spoke many languages. But all were called Seminoles. The chief of Tiger's Seminole town was Billy Bowlegs.

Tilly and her family ferried home across the Suwannee River. Tilly carried the cooking pot.

The black families lived in Nero's Town, a village about a mile from Bowlegs Town. Most of them had escaped from slavery in the Carolinas, Georgia, or Florida. They became known as black Seminoles.

Many of the black Seminoles in Nero's Town lived as free people. But some of them had been sold to Chief Bowlegs.

The village was governed by a man named Nero. Chief Bowlegs allowed Nero to run the village as he saw fit.

Kwaku had built a roomy wooden cabin for his family in Nero's Town. The cabin was larger and sturdier than Tiger's house in Bowlegs Town.

"Chief Bowlegs is nothing like Master Miller," Tilly said on the way home.

"I wish I had a coin for every time you've said that," her father teased.

"But it's true," Tilly said. "Master Miller made his slaves live where he lives. And Master Miller didn't let slaves have land. He didn't let them own horses, pigs, and cows either."

"You don't have to call him 'master' anymore," Catbird told her.

"That's another thing," Tilly went on. "Chief Bowlegs doesn't make his slaves say 'master.' He doesn't have an overseer watching them all the time. He never has them punished." Tilly shivered at the thought of cruel Mr. Stroud.

"Everything you say is true," Kwaku agreed.

"I don't understand," Tilly went on. "Chief Bowlegs doesn't mind if his slaves travel out of town. They don't even have to ask first. The men can take their rifles and hunt deer in the woods. They seem as free as we are. So why does Chief Bowlegs say he owns them?"

"Maybe you should ask Tiger," Catbird suggested.

Tilly wasn't sure she was brave enough to do that. She might ask Tiger's mother, though. Tilly and Catbird visited her often in Bowlegs Town.

On one such visit, they sat outdoors sewing. Catbird and Tiger's mother talked on and on in Yuchi. At last they ran out of things to say.

Tilly was about to ask her question when she heard

pounding hooves. She turned to see Mr. Miller and Mr. Stroud riding into the village. Terror grabbed Tilly's heart.

"Mother, look!" Tilly cried.

"Oh, no!" Catbird exclaimed. "Tilly, hurry. We must hide. They may not have seen us yet."

But it was too late. Mr. Stroud was pointing at them. The two men galloped closer. They reined in their horses. Catbird put her arms around Tilly. Tilly could feel her mother shaking.

Indian Seminole men began to gather nearby. Each carried a rifle. Tiger stepped forward.

"Why have you come?" he asked.

"This woman and her daughter are my property," Mr. Miller said. "I've come to take them back."

"He owns her husband too," Mr. Stroud added. "Where is he?"

"Can you prove that you own them?" Tiger asked.

Mr. Stroud got down from his horse. "We don't have to prove anything to you!" he shouted.

"Turn them over to us now!" Mr. Miller ordered.

The Indian Seminole men formed a line. Guns ready, they stood in Mr. Stroud's way.

"The woman and child stay here," Tiger said.

Mr. Stroud looked at Mr. Miller.

"Today you have us outnumbered," Mr. Miller growled. "But we'll return with more men. I will reclaim what's mine."

Mr. Stroud remounted. He and Mr. Miller turned their horses and thundered away.

Tilly and Catbird sank to the ground. Tilly burst into tears. Tiger came over and patted her hair.

"The danger has passed," he said.

Tilly lifted her head to look at him.

"Why didn't you let them take us back?" she asked.

Tiger sat down beside her. "For more than 100 years, escaped slaves have lived among us," he explained. "They've been the friends of Indians all that time. Many of them have married Indians. They've taught us to be better farmers. From them we've learned to build better houses."

"They also know the white people's language," Tiger's mother added. "They translate for us. Escaped slaves give us good advice about dealing with white people."

Tilly thought for a moment. Then she asked, "If they've done so much for you, why don't you set them free?"

"Many people in your town *are* free," Tiger reminded her.

"I know," Tilly said. "But some still belong to your chief. Why not set those people free?"

Instead of answering, Tiger asked a question. "Did you know that Bowlegs Town was not always here on the Suwannee River?"

"I didn't know that," Tilly said. She wondered why Tiger had changed the subject.

"About three years ago, our town was miles away," Tiger said. "Then white men from Georgia and Tennessee attacked us. They burned our houses. We had harvested almost 2,000 bushels of corn. The white men ate or destroyed all of it. They took 300 horses and 400 head of cattle from us. They stole 2,000 deerskins."

"That's horrible," Tilly said.

"We fought them as best we could," Tiger added. "Twenty Seminoles died in the fighting. Nine were captured. Some of those captured were black. We came here to rebuild our town."

"That's very sad," Tilly said. "Why did those white men attack you?"

"Your former master was angry today," Tiger said. "Those men from Georgia and Tennessee were angry too. They didn't want escaped slaves to live with Seminoles. They were afraid all their slaves would run away and hide among us."

"But what does that story have to do with my question?" Tilly asked, confused.

"The story is the answer to your question," Tiger told her. "White people are already angry. Suppose Seminoles set all slaves free. How do you think the white people would feel?"

"Even more angry?" Tilly asked.

"That's right. So Seminole chiefs hold slaves," Tiger went on. "That way the white people are a little less afraid of Seminoles putting an end to slavery."

"And they are a little less angry," Tilly guessed.

"You figure things out quickly," Tiger said. "Chief Bowlegs doesn't ask much of the people he owns. Each slave family gives him ten bushels of corn at harvesttime. Each slave family also gives one hog or a side of beef every year. That leaves plenty for the family to eat."

"My family gives Chief Bowlegs corn and meat too," Tilly said.

"The food from Nero's village makes Bowlegs Town wealthier. When we are well-off, we can protect you better."

"The way you did today?" Tilly asked.

"Yes." Tiger shook his head. "The plantation owners won't give up easily."

"Enough serious talk," Tiger's mother broke in. "You'll frighten her."

"My mother is right, as usual," Tiger said. "And my talk of corn reminds me that it's almost harvesttime. Tilly, you and your parents will be my guests at the green corn festival."

6

Harvest Celebration

"How much longer, Mother?" Tilly asked.

"If you don't sit still, I'll have to start over," Catbird said.

"I don't want to miss anything," Tilly told her.

"The green corn festival lasts four days," her mother reminded her. "Don't you want your hair to look nice?"

Seminoles dressed in their very best for the green corn festival, or *busk*. Since settling in Nero's village, Tilly and her family never wore "Negro cloth."

Kwaku now dressed in a long, loose, belted Seminole shirt and scarves. For the busk, he would add a turban decorated with feathers.

Like other Seminole women, Catbird and Tilly wore blouses and long skirts. Today they wrapped yards of beads around their necks. Catbird's hair was already woven into a fancy style. She was hurrying to finish Tilly's hair.

The new corn was picked in early summer. At the full moon in July, the Seminoles rejoiced. They feasted and danced at the busk. Some of the dancing was just for fun. Other dances were part of important rituals.

The ritual dancers tied shells around their ankles. They stomped to drumbeats while medicine men passed around a black drink. The black drink was a tea brewed from the leaves of a bush.

The sacred Feather Dance would also be performed. The dancers would hold the feathers of a white heron.

On the third morning of the busk, priests would bring out medicine bundles. That night, the bundles would be opened. The contents of the bundles would be hidden again at dawn.

The busk was also a time for new beginnings. Trials were held. People forgave old debts. Arguments were settled. No grudges were to be carried over into the new year.

"Are you ready?" Kwaku called out.

"Just finished," Catbird answered.

Kwaku stepped into the cabin. "Never before have I seen two such beautiful ladies," he declared.

Kwaku offered one arm to Tilly and one to Catbird. "I can't wait to show you off at Bowlegs Town," he said.

🌿 🌿 🌿

Four days later, Tilly sat watching a huge bonfire. Tiger's mother sat beside her. The fire crackled in the square ground in the center of town. People were burning worn-out clothing and furniture. They had bought new things to replace the old.

Earlier that day, the new corn from the harvest had been eaten for the first time. The busk was almost over.

"I think the last day is my favorite," Tilly said.

"Aren't you going to dance some more?" Tiger's mother asked.

"I'm too tired to dance another step," Tilly sighed.

Tiger's mother chuckled. "Your parents have more energy than you do," she said. "They're still dancing."

"Father can't get enough of the stomp dancing," Tilly said. "It reminds him of dancing in West Africa."

Tilly watched her parents in the glow of the firelight. They looked so happy. Tilly's heart was filled with gladness as well. People here never looked down their noses at her. She couldn't imagine a better place to be.

🌿 🌿 🌿

Some weeks later, Tilly was helping Kwaku repair the garden fence. The fence kept pigs and cattle from grazing on the fruit and vegetables.

Nero's wife rode into the yard.

"Is Catbird home?" she asked.

"Yes," Kwaku replied. "Just go on in."

Nero's wife was inside for a very short time. Then she came out with Catbird.

"I'll be gone for a while," Catbird said.

"Where are you going?" Tilly asked.

"There's been an attack on Fort Mosa," Nero's wife explained. "The fort was blown up, and people were burned. Survivors fled to our town. Help is needed in nursing them."

"We'd better go right away," Catbird said.

"I've never heard of Fort Mosa," Tilly said after the two women rode away.

"It's near St. Augustine," her father told her. "The fort was built by the British. After a while, they left. Then black families stayed there and helped defend St. Augustine."

"Who attacked the fort?" Tilly asked.

"I don't know. We'll learn more when your mother returns," Kwaku said.

Catbird brought home a guest for supper. The man with her was thin and very tall. His face was wide and square. He looked to be about 25 years old. Tilly tried hard not to stare at his crossed right eye.

"This is Abraham," Catbird said. "Until now, he has lived at Fort Mosa."

"Who attacked your home?" Tilly asked.

"Abraham will tell us what happened soon enough," Kwaku said. "First let him rest and eat."

After supper, the family listened to Abraham's story. His voice was soft and low. Yet he spoke each word clearly.

Like Kwaku, Abraham had been captured in West Africa. He'd been the slave of a doctor. In 1814, he learned that the British army wanted slaves to enlist. Those who signed up would be set free. So Abraham escaped and joined the British troops.

"Life at Fort Mosa was good for former slaves," Abraham said. "Slave owners in the United States couldn't stand that. Neither could some members of their government. They wouldn't leave us alone."

"But Florida isn't part of the United States," Catbird said.

"True," Abraham replied. "But it is right next to America. Slaves from America can easily run here. So American planters fear losing all their slaves."

"They couldn't *all* run away," Tilly said.

"The Americans believe those who have escaped might secretly return," Abraham told her.

"Why?" Tilly asked.

"To get all slaves to rise up against their owners," Abraham explained.

"What a wonderful idea," Kwaku said.

"Yes, it is," Abraham said. "But we had no such plan. There weren't enough of us to start a revolt. We were too busy looking out for ourselves."

"But many Americans didn't want you living there," Catbird said.

"That's right," Abraham told them. "They also want to take Florida away from Spain. So the United States Army marched against us. Five hundred Creek Indians marched with them. General Andrew Jackson ordered the attack. We were to be captured and returned to slavery."

"I'm sure you all fought fiercely," Kwaku said.

"If only we had been able to fight longer. But the fort stood on a river," Abraham explained. "The United States Navy sent ships up the river. Hot shot from the ships flew into the fort. One of the red-hot cannon balls landed where the gunpowder was stored. The explosion was huge."

"Did that end the battle?" Tilly asked.

"Oh, yes," Abraham told her. "Almost everyone was killed or injured. The fort was destroyed." Abraham stopped speaking. He heaved a deep sigh and shook his head.

"You don't have to tell us any more," Kwaku said. "I'm sure it's very painful to think about."

"You're welcome to stay here tonight," Catbird offered.

"You're very kind," Abraham said. "But I must go and check on those who came here with me."

Kwaku escorted Abraham back to Nero's house. Tilly helped her mother clean up. Suddenly Tilly gasped.

"What's wrong?" Catbird asked.

"I just had a terrible thought," Tilly said. "What if we had made it to St. Augustine? We might have ended up living at Fort Mosa."

Catbird couldn't say anything. She just nodded.

"Mother," Tilly asked, "will General Jackson attack us too?"

"I hope not," Catbird sighed.

♨ ♨ ♨

As time went by, Kwaku and Abraham became fast friends. Abraham often visited the house. Tilly listened as he and Kwaku shared memories of West Africa.

They also talked about the right of every person to be free.

"I will resist anyone who tries to recapture me," Abraham said one day. He, Tilly, and Kwaku talked while Catbird finished getting ready for a wedding in town.

"If I'm taken anyway, I'll escape again," Abraham said. "I'll escape as often as I must. And I'll help others to remain free. We deserve to be as free as the white slave owners."

"They aren't as free as they think," Kwaku said.

"What do you mean, Father?" Tilly asked.

"Slave owners are ruled by their need to keep others in slavery," Kwaku said. "Mr. Miller became a slave to punishing us. He could chain my body. But I was a free man in spirit."

Catbird had been listening while she braided her hair. But now she said, "It's time to leave for the wedding."

"We'd better hurry," Tilly said. "We don't want to miss the jumping over."

Tilly remembered "jumping over" from the plantation. The father of the groom held one end of a stick. The bride's father held the other end. The groom jumped over the stick first. Next the bride jumped over. And that was how they were married.

Everyone in Nero's Town would be at the wedding. A big party with plenty of food would follow.

"You're almost 14 now," Abraham said to Tilly on the way to the wedding. "Are you sweet on a boy yet?"

Tilly giggled. "Not on *a* boy. There are three I like. I can't make up my mind."

"You have plenty of time to decide," Abraham told her.

At the moment, it seemed as if there would be plenty of time for all good things to come.

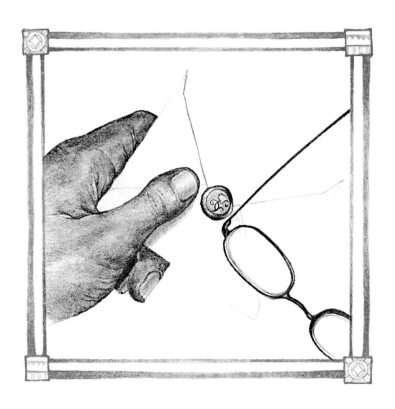

7

The Letter

The year 1818 began peacefully in Nero's Town. The calm lasted just over three months.

The April air was fresh and breezy. Worrying was a waste of such a beautiful day. But Tilly couldn't help worrying.

She was waiting for her parents to come home. Nero's village was nearly empty. Almost everyone had gone to the Suwannee River Trading Post.

The trading post had been opened early in 1817 by Alexander Arbuthnot. Mr. Arbuthnot was from Scotland. The Seminoles took corn, hides, and beeswax to the trading post. In return, they got cloth, household goods, and guns.

Black and Indian Seminoles trusted Mr. Arbuthnot. In June of 1817, they had named him their agent. He wrote letters for them to the governments of Britain, Spain, and the United States.

Right now Mr. Arbuthnot was away visiting the Spanish fort at St. Marks. He had just sent a letter to the trading post. Chief Bowlegs' people had been called to the trading post. Nero's people had been sent for as well. At the trading post, the letter would be read to them.

Tilly was sure the letter contained bad news. By staying home, she could delay learning what it was.

But she couldn't put off knowing forever. Her parents soon returned.

"General Jackson is marching into Florida," Kwaku told her. "He's leading a powerful army. He'll come east to the Suwannee River. He wants to destroy Bowlegs Town and our settlement."

"But this land belongs to Spain," Tilly said. "Won't the Spaniards stop him?"

"They are no match for Jackson's troops," Kwaku said.

"Why doesn't General Jackson leave us alone?" Tilly asked. "We haven't caused any trouble."

"American slave owners are afraid of us," Kwaku said. "We live in a large group. We run our own lives. That scares them. They won't rest until every black person is a slave again."

Tilly began to tremble. "What are we going to do?" she cried.

Kwaku put his arm around Tilly's shoulders. "Try to stay calm," he said. "Nero and Chief Bowlegs will talk things over and form a plan."

Tilly was shocked when she heard the plan. Chief Bowlegs would take his people to hide in the swamp. The women and children of Nero's Town would be ferried across the river. They would take cover on the eastern side. The black Seminole men would stay on the western shore to fight General Jackson's army.

Tilly remembered Tiger saying that the Indian Seminoles would protect the black Seminoles.

"How can Chief Bowlegs leave us like that?" she asked.

"Some of his warriors will stay to help us," Catbird said.

"They should *all* stay," Tilly grumbled. "They should all protect us."

"Chief Bowlegs has given us something better," Kwaku said. "He won't force us to do what he's decided. He'll let us decide for ourselves—as free people do."

"We'd better get busy," Catbird said. "We have a lot of packing to do."

Before Tilly's family packed their own belongings, they helped other people. Black Seminoles who were sick or very old would cross the river first. Women with young babies would then get to safety.

Tilly was glad to help. But General Jackson's troops drew nearer every moment. Tilly feared that she and her mother wouldn't get out in time.

After a few days, Tiger showed up in Nero's village. He set aside his gun and pitched in with the packing.

Tilly walked over to him.

"You didn't desert us," she whispered.

Tiger's eyebrows shot up in surprise. "Of course not," he said.

At last Tilly and her mother were packing their own belongings. Tiger wasn't helping them that day. He and five other Seminole warriors were on a scouting mission. They were trying to locate General Jackson's troops.

"Should I bring this blouse?" Catbird asked Tilly. "You've almost outgrown it."

"It doesn't matter," Tilly said. "Just leave it. Please hurry, Mother. It's already the middle of the afternoon. We're not even half finished."

Catbird sighed. "I wish your father were here."

Kwaku was practicing drills with the other Black Seminole fighters.

Just then Tilly heard shouting. She looked outside. Tiger was riding hard toward the cabin. He pulled his horse up sharply in front of the door.

"Jackson's army is about six miles away," he warned. "You and your mother must get down to the river now."

Tilly grabbed the door frame. Her head spun. She thought she might faint.

"Be brave, Tilly," she heard Tiger say. "Help your mother."

Then he was galloping away.

"Be brave," Tilly repeated to herself. She went back inside and picked up two bundles. "Let's go, Mother," she said.

"We can't carry everything in one trip," Catbird said.

"You heard Tiger," Tilly cried. "We don't have much time. We'll have to leave some of it."

"You're right," Catbird replied. "Things can always be replaced." She filled her arms with bundles.

The ferry landing was a madhouse. Villagers left

many of their belongings behind on the shore. At this last frantic moment, people were more important than property.

Tilly and Catbird waited for their turn. The sun dropped below the treetops. Its rays winked between the branches. Still they waited.

The sun slipped out of sight. A halo of soft red light glowed above the trees. At last Tilly and Catbird stepped onto the ferry.

A volley of shots rang out. Everyone on the ferry turned to look. More gunfire exploded on the western side of the river. Flashes of light filled the air. Clouds of smoke began to rise above the underbrush.

The ferry moved away from the fighting. One thought took over Tilly's mind—Father is back there!

She didn't remember deciding to jump into the water. Yet she found herself swimming back toward the shore. She heard her mother calling her name. Still she splashed closer to the bank.

Dripping, Tilly climbed onto dry land. She knew only that she had to find her father. What if he didn't live through the battle? Nero had only 300 warriors. How could they defeat the thousands led by General Jackson?

Tilly dashed toward the sounds of fighting. Suddenly a bullet whizzed past her. Tilly dropped to her knees and began crawling.

The rifle shots grew louder. The light grew dimmer. Smoke rolled toward Tilly. She could hardly see. What had she been thinking? She would never find her father in this confusion. Should she return to the river? How would she get across?

All at once, someone rushed toward her. Tilly lay flat. The man stumbled over her and fell. In the smoky dusk, Tilly squinted at him. It was Abraham!

Should Tilly help him up? She knew he would be furious with her. Instead she scrambled behind a bush. Abraham got to his feet and looked at the ground around him. Then he shrugged, picked up his rifle, and moved on.

Darkness had now fallen. Tilly realized that she was lost. Which way was the river?

The gunfire began to die down. Figures moved past Tilly in the night.

"Jackson's men won't follow us after dark," Tilly heard a man say. Tilly recognized the voice. He was her neighbor.

The black Seminole fighters were withdrawing to the river. Tilly crept along with them. Soon her head was one of hundreds bobbing in the Suwannee. Arm over arm, she swam for the safety of the far shore.

8

On the Run

"I should have your hide, young lady," Catbird said. Tilly quaked under her mother's burning gaze. "How could you act so crazy? You nearly frightened me to death."

"Please don't be mad, Mother," Tilly begged. "You're right. What I did was stupid. I'm sorry."

"I had to worry about both you and your father," Catbird went on.

After swimming the river, Tilly had slept soaking wet on the bare ground. She didn't know where the families had camped.

Her mother had found her at dawn. First Catbird had hugged Tilly and wrapped her in a blanket. Now she was scolding her daughter.

"I'm sorry, Mother," Tilly said again. "I don't know what made me do it. I was just so afraid Father would get killed. Have you seen him?"

"Not yet," Catbird said.

Weary warriors were stretched out everywhere. Tilly and her mother picked their way among them. They couldn't find Kwaku. Tears flowed from their eyes.

"Why are my two special ladies crying?" Tilly's heart leapt at the sound of her father's voice.

She flung herself at him, dropping her blanket. "Where have you been?" she cried.

"I was searching for you and your mother," he said. He turned to Catbird.

"Why aren't you with the other women and children? And why are Tilly's clothes all wet?"

"I'll explain later," Catbird said, dabbing at her

eyes. "Right now, Tilly needs something dry to wear."

"I wonder where Tiger is," Tilly said. "I hope he wasn't hurt."

"He's fine," Kwaku told her. "He's gone to report to Chief Bowlegs."

That morning, Abraham gave a speech. First he praised the warriors.

"Every man fought bravely," he said. "You did all you could in our defense. We will forever honor the memory of those who died."

Many in the crowd began to weep.

"Sadly, Nero is no longer among us," Abraham told them.

Wails of sorrow rose from the crowd. Abraham was silent for a moment.

"Jackson will send soldiers after us," Abraham went on at last. "We must move farther from the river. For now, we must break up into small bands. We must go in many directions. Tracking us will be harder that way."

The crying began again.

"Jackson's men cannot follow us for long," Abraham said. "In time we'll gather together once more. We'll start a new town in another place."

The refugees from Nero's Town began walking. They said good-bye as groups of people went their separate ways. With each farewell, Tilly fought back tears.

Behind them, clouds of gray smoke filled the sky. Bowlegs Town and Nero's Town were being burned to the ground.

As they traveled, Kwaku spoke about the battle.

"There were too many of them," he said. "And their weapons have a greater range than ours."

"Did you see any white soldiers up close?" Tilly asked.

"The men I was fighting were Creek Indians," Kwaku told her.

"Didn't Creek Indians help the Americans at Fort Mosa too?" Tilly asked.

"That's right," Abraham said. Tilly was glad Abraham had stayed with them. She still felt guilty about tripping him in the dark.

The group stopped in the middle of the afternoon. One man in their party was wounded and hobbled along slowly. They had covered only about three miles.

Everyone needed to rest and eat. Catbird had some corn and a pot in one of the bundles. Tilly built a fire, and Catbird cooked the corn. Abraham was invited to join them.

"Something strange happened to me during the battle," he said as they ate. "I stumbled over someone lying on the ground. I thought it must be one of our men who had been hit. But after I got up, no one was there."

"Maybe it was one of the Creeks," Catbird suggested. "He could have gotten up and slipped away."

"Perhaps," Abraham said. "Whoever it was helped me greatly."

"What do you mean?" Tilly asked.

"Just as I fell, a bullet zinged over my head," Abraham told them. "If I hadn't gone down, I surely would have been killed."

Tilly couldn't help smiling. She felt much better about her reckless adventure near the Suwannee.

❦ ❦ ❦

The next day, the group walked another couple of miles. Tilly was glad when they stopped by a stream. She'd never felt so tired.

The corn Catbird had brought was almost gone. Others in the group had no corn left at all. The refugees had to begin gathering China briar root.

From the roots they would make *koontie*, or red flour, for bread. The washed roots would be pounded and soaked. The pulp would then be drained and fermented. Next it would be spread on palmetto leaves to dry. Once dry, the red flour could be made into bread. The process took many days.

"Jackson has driven us away from our cornfields," Kwaku said. "But we won't starve. Besides the koontie, we can live on the cabbage of the palmetto. We can also roast acorns from live oak trees."

"After the koontie is ready, we should move on," Abraham said. "Jackson's scouts might still be in the area."

Everyone in the group agreed. The farther they got from the Suwannee River, the safer they would be.

But Tilly felt weaker each day. Her head began to hurt. Her throat was sore.

"I can't get up," she said one morning. "I'm just too tired."

Catbird felt her daughter's forehead. "You have a fever," she said.

Tilly went back to sleep. When she woke up, her eyes burned. The world looked blurry. She drifted off again.

A dim shape appeared in front of Tilly's eyes. "Father?" Tilly whispered.

"No, Tilly, it's Abraham. I'm here to say good-bye."

Tilly tried to ask why. Her voice stuck in her swollen throat.

"Don't try to talk," Abraham said. "You are very sick. The rest of the group is moving on. You're too ill to travel. Your parents will nurse you here."

Tilly shook her head. She grabbed at Abraham's shirt.

"This is not good-bye forever," Abraham said. "Your mother and father know where we are headed. In a few days, you will be stronger. Then your family can catch up with us. We'll see each other again soon."

Abraham squeezed Tilly's hand. Then he was gone.

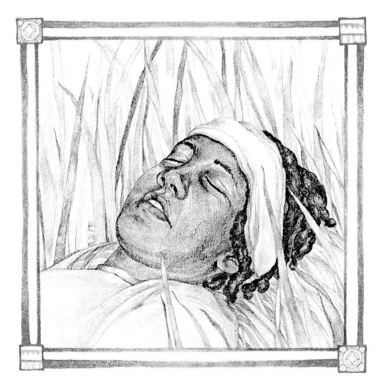

9

A Nightmare

Tilly's world was taken over by wild dreams. Sights and sounds swirled around her. It was difficult to tell what was real and what wasn't.

Tilly's fever raged. Her ears rang. One moment she shivered under her blanket. The next moment she was covered in sweat.

Her parents trickled water into her mouth. They washed her face with a cool, damp cloth.

How long had she been sick? Had she been lying here for hours or days? Day and night blended into one.

Catbird's voice sang softly. A wet cloth was pressed against Tilly's forehead. Suddenly she heard a thundering sound. Then her father shouted, and her mother screamed.

Tilly was lifted by strong arms and carried. She heard the voices of men she didn't know. They spoke words she couldn't understand. Horses snorted and stamped nearby. How she hated these fever nightmares.

Hands grabbed Tilly roughly. She was slung facedown across the back of a horse. A rider mounted and urged the animal forward.

This was no dream. Tilly bounced against the horse's shoulders. Pain filled every part of her body. Her stomach heaved and she gagged. Then she passed out.

Voices broke through the fog in Tilly's head. She had to see what was going on. But her eyes would barely open. Shadowy forms shifted in front of her. Were the shadows her parents? She tried to call to them. A feeble croak came out of her throat.

"I'm here, Tilly," her father's voice whispered.

Feeling safer, Tilly let her eyelids fall closed. She slept again.

When she awoke, her mother spoke to her. "Drink a little, Tilly." The cool water soothed Tilly's dry mouth.

"Where are we?" Tilly mumbled.

"Don't worry," Catbird said. "Just rest."

Soon Tilly dozed off again. Mr. Stroud haunted her sleep. He stood over her, laughing coldly. The dreadful sound wouldn't go away. What a cruel illness this was.

Next Tilly was being jolted and bounced. She forced her eyes open. She could just make out boards near her head. Horseshoes thudded and wooden wheels creaked. Had Tiger come in his wagon to rescue them? The curtain of sleep closed over the world once more.

A woman's voice sang softly. A wet cloth was pressed against Tilly's forehead. Relief flooded through Tilly. She had dreamed everything after all. She was still lying by the stream getting better. Soon she and her family would join the others from Nero's Town again.

Tilly's head began to clear. She realized that the voice was not her mother's. Yet Tilly knew the voice well. She opened her eyes. A blurred brown face hovered above her. Slowly the face came into focus.

Tilly was gazing up at Samantha.

At first Tilly wept for joy.

"Oh, Samantha," she murmured. "I missed you so much. Is Samson here too?"

"Of course he is," Samantha said.

"How did you get here?" Tilly asked. "How did you find us?"

"Whatever do you mean, child?" Samantha sounded surprised. Tilly opened her eyes wide. As she looked around, she let out a horrified cry. She was in Samantha and Samson's cabin on the Miller Plantation.

"How did I get here?" Tilly asked.

"Creek Indian scouts searched for miles around Bowlegs Town," Samantha told her. "They found you and your parents while you were sick."

"Where are my parents?" Tilly asked.

"Right now they are working in the fields," Samantha said.

Tilly began to sob miserably. Samantha hugged her tightly and rocked back and forth.

After a while, Tilly grew calmer. "How did the Creek scouts know to bring us here?" she asked.

"They didn't," Samantha replied. "Master Miller had learned about the defeat of your town. He sent Mr. Stroud and some other men to the area. They met up with the scouts. Mr. Stroud paid them a reward and got the three of you back."

"Are my parents all right?" Tilly asked.

"Yes, they are." Samantha looked away.

"Will they be coming in from work soon? I want to see them."

"I'm afraid you can't," Samantha said.

"Why not? Why can't I see them?" Tilly asked.

"They're being punished for escaping. They must go straight to the cell after their work is done. They sleep there chained to the wall every night."

Tilly began to cry harder than ever.

"Hush, child, hush," Samantha said. "Your fever will come back if you carry on so."

But Tilly couldn't stop wailing. Sobs shook her until she wore herself out. Finally, she slept in Samantha's arms.

Day after day, Samantha and Samson cared tenderly for Tilly. In spite of her sorrow, Tilly sat up and sipped some broth. Later, she was able to eat corn mush.

Tilly told Samantha and Samson all about the past few years. There was too much to tell all at once. They heard the story a little at a time.

One day, Tilly heard a horse trot up and stop outside the cabin. A young woman stepped inside. At first Tilly didn't know who she was. Then the young woman spoke.

"Are you feeling better, Tilly?" she asked.

"Lydia?" Tilly said.

"Of course," Lydia laughed. "Who did you think?"

"You look so grown-up," Tilly answered. "You're taller. And you don't have ringlets anymore."

"You look grown-up yourself," Lydia told her.

"What can we do for you, Miss Lydia?" Samantha asked.

"I've come to take Tilly for a ride," Lydia said. "She's been in bed long enough. She needs some fresh air."

Tilly didn't want to go outside. Her Seminole clothes had been taken away. She was once again wearing the hated slave dress.

But Tilly knew she couldn't refuse Lydia. Samson and Samantha helped Tilly out of bed. Hanging on to them, she wobbled to the cabin door.

When Tilly saw Lydia's chestnut mare, she felt more like riding. "What a beautiful horse," Tilly said.

Tilly patted the horse's sleek reddish brown neck. The animal turned her head and nuzzled Tilly gently.

"She's a present from Father," Lydia said.

Lydia got into the saddle. Tilly was helped up behind her. The horse started off at a walk. The breeze and sunshine felt good.

Lydia began to visit Tilly almost every day. They'd ride out to a meadow and sit under a tree.

"Why are you being so nice to me?" Tilly asked Lydia one afternoon.

"This is your new job," Lydia told her. "There's no one around here my age. I get lonely. So I asked for you as my companion."

"You asked to spend time with a 'lowly zambo'?" Tilly asked in surprise.

Lydia looked down at her lap. "I wish I'd never said that. I know better now."

"Your parents don't mind?" Tilly asked.

"A little," Lydia answered. "But they always give me what I want."

"Can you get them to stop punishing my parents?" Tilly asked.

"I don't think so. Father doesn't let anyone tell him how to run the plantation."

🌿 🌿 🌿

A few days later, Lydia brought a package with her to the cabin.

"What's that?" Tilly asked as they mounted the chestnut mare.

"I'll show you when we get to the tree," Lydia said.

In the shade of spreading branches, Lydia opened the brown paper wrapping. Tilly saw the book she had once taken from the kitchen table.

"I'm going to teach you to read," Lydia declared.

"We can't do that!" Tilly exclaimed. "We'd be breaking the rules."

"No one has to know."

"I still don't want to," Tilly said. "I don't want anything to do with that book. I hate it. My father almost got sold because of it."

"What do you mean?" Lydia asked. "Father would never sell Kwaku. He always says that your father is worth three other slaves. That's why he lets your father keep his African name."

"But Mr. Stroud showed me the paper ordering the sale of my father," Tilly said.

Lydia laughed. "Mr. Stroud always uses that trick to scare slaves. There was no such order. He might have waved a shopping list in front of you. He knew you couldn't read it."

Rage welled up in Tilly. She no longer feared breaking the rule. Never again would she be so helpless.

"Please teach me," Tilly said.

10

A Big Mistake

Every day, Lydia and Tilly sat with the book between them. Tilly learned the names of the letters and their sounds. Then she learned the sounds made by groups of letters. Soon words began to take shape.

Tilly's new knowledge filled her with a sense of power. Yet her mind often wandered.

"You're not listening," Lydia said one day. "What are you thinking about?"

"My parents," Tilly sighed. "I miss them so much."

"Haven't you seen them at all?" Lydia asked.

"Once or twice," Tilly said. "I hid by the cell at dawn. I saw them when Mr. Stroud let them out for work. But I couldn't speak to them."

"Maybe I'll talk to Father about it," Lydia said. "But I have to wait until he's in a really good mood."

That night, Tilly told Samantha and Samson what Lydia had said.

"I hope she can change her father's mind," Samson said.

"So do I," Tilly said. "Mother and Father must be so miserable. Their life here is so much harder than it was before. And they had grown used to being free."

"I can't imagine how the three of you must feel," Samantha said. "You tasted freedom. Now it has been taken away again."

"It might have been better if you'd never escaped," Samson added.

"Oh, no!" Tilly exclaimed. "I'll never feel that way. I wish you and Samantha had been with us. I wish you could know how wonderful freedom is. You deserve to find out before you leave this earth."

Samantha and Samson looked at each other in silence.

🌿 🌿 🌿

Lydia didn't show up at the cabin the next day. The following day, the cook's son brought Tilly a message.

"Miss Lydia sent me from the big house," he said. "She wants you to know she's sick."

"Is she very ill?" Tilly asked.

"No," the child answered. "She said you might see her tomorrow."

Tilly thanked the little boy. He ran off up the road.

"Do you think I should try to visit Lydia?" Tilly asked Samantha.

"That would be nice," Samantha said. "You could go to the kitchen door and ask."

"I will," Tilly said. But as she walked toward the big house, she had an idea. She could go out to the fields and try to find her parents. Hugging them just once would do her so much good.

Tilly walked across the meadow and past the big tree. All at once, she heard hoofbeats behind her. Had Lydia come outdoors after all?

Tilly turned her head to see Mr. Stroud riding after her. She kept walking. He drew up beside her and slowed his horse.

"Where do you think you're going?" he snarled.

"I'm taking a walk."

"I forbid it," he growled. "Turn around and go back to your cabin."

"I'm Miss Lydia's friend now," Tilly said. "She'll be mad if you're mean to me."

"Miss Lydia doesn't own you," Mr. Stroud said. "Her father owns you. And I answer to him. Now do as I say."

Tilly stopped walking but did not turn around.

"You'd better obey me," Mr. Stroud warned. "Or would you rather be sold away from your family?"

"Mr. Miller would never do that," Tilly said. "Miss Lydia wouldn't let him."

"How dare you sass me?" Mr. Stroud snapped. He took a sheet of paper out of his pocket. "This order was written by Mr. Miller. It says to sell you if you get uppity."

Mr. Stroud dangled the paper in front of Tilly. Her eyes flew over the page. She spotted the word *apples*. In another place she saw *cup of flour*. *Sugar*, she read silently. She picked out the words *oven* and *bake*.

"That paper's not about me!" Tilly shouted. "It's a recipe for apple pie!"

Tilly clapped her hand over her mouth. She'd just made a terrible mistake.

Mr. Stroud glared at her. "How would you know that?" he asked.

"I don't," Tilly said quickly. "I—I was just guessing. I'm going to do what you said now. I'm going home."

Tilly began to run. Would Mr. Stroud come after her? Would he grab her and drag her to Mr. Miller? After a moment, Tilly dared to look back. Mr. Stroud was still sitting on his horse watching her go.

Slowing to a walk, Tilly covered a few more yards. She looked back again. Mr. Stroud had turned his horse and was riding away.

Tilly sat down in the grass to think. Mr. Stroud wouldn't believe that she'd guessed the words. He wasn't that big a fool. And he would tell Mr. Miller as soon as he got the chance.

"Why was I such an idiot?" Tilly moaned. "Why didn't I keep quiet? What am I going to do now?"

A minute later, Tilly jumped up. She would try to visit Lydia after all. Lydia should be warned—and maybe she could help.

Tilly hurried to the big house. She knocked on the kitchen door. The cook peered out through the screen.

"Would you please find out if I may see Miss Lydia?" Tilly asked.

The cook looked her up and down. "I'm very busy right now," she said.

"Please," Tilly begged. "I thought she might need cheering up."

The cook grunted. "Wait there," she said.

Before long, the cook came back. She held open the screen door for Tilly.

"Go on upstairs," she said.

Tilly had never been beyond the kitchen of the big house.

"How will I know which room?" she asked.

"Miss Lydia will be waiting in her doorway," the cook said.

On any other day, Tilly would have been awed by the house. She walked over soft rugs. Paintings in fancy frames hung on the walls. Fine china vases stood on carved oak tables.

But today Tilly was too worried to notice the luxury around her. She hurried up the broad staircase.

"Over here," Lydia said when she saw Tilly.

They went into Lydia's room and sat in plush armchairs. Frilly curtains fluttered in the breeze.

"How are you?" Tilly asked.

"Much better," Lydia said. "I'm glad you came. Being stuck in bed is boring."

"I hope you aren't very sick," Tilly said.

"Oh, no. It's just a cold." Then Lydia spoke in a whisper. "Should I get out the book?"

Tilly shook her head. "Not today. I have to talk to you. I've done the most foolish thing."

"I'm sure it can't be that bad," Lydia said.

"Oh, but it is." Her voice shaking, Tilly told Lydia what had happened.

"That *is* bad," Lydia said when Tilly finished.

"I didn't tell Mr. Stroud you taught me," Tilly added.

"My father might suspect," Lydia said. "But he has no proof. I won't get in trouble. We have to decide what you should do."

The two girls talked for a long while. Together they formed a plan.

At last, Lydia put on a robe over her nightgown. She and Tilly went down to the kitchen.

"Do we have any day-old bread?" Lydia asked the cook.

"Yes, Miss Lydia," the cook replied. "There are two loaves in the pantry."

"I'm giving them to Tilly," Lydia said. "Tomorrow we're going to feed the birds in the meadow."

"Very good, Miss Lydia," the cook said.

"I'll give her some fruit too," Lydia went on. "That way we'll have something to snack on."

Tilly left the kitchen carrying a cloth bag. Lydia followed her onto the porch. She gave Tilly a quick hug.

"Good luck," she whispered in Tilly's ear.

"Thank you," Tilly said. "You're a real friend."

That night at bedtime, Tilly squeezed Samantha tightly.

"I love you," Tilly said.

Next she hugged Samson.

"I love you too," she told him. "Thank you both for taking care of me."

"It's a joy having you with us," Samantha told her.

Tilly could hardly keep from crying. But she couldn't let Samantha and Samson in on the plan. She didn't want to place them in danger.

Tilly didn't sleep a wink that night.

11

A Second Chance

Before dawn, Tilly tiptoed out of the cabin. She carried the cloth bag full of bread and fruit. She also brought her hat with the wide brim.

Near the cell, Tilly hid behind a bush. She waited for the morning bell to ring. As the bell clanged, Mr. Stroud appeared. He unlocked the cell door. Then he went in to unfasten the chains. Catbird stepped out first, followed by Kwaku.

Tilly wanted to call out to them. But she'd already made too many mistakes. She bit her lip and kept silent.

Mr. Stroud handed each of Tilly's parents a bowl. "Make it snappy," he ordered.

Tilly watched her mother and father eat their cooked cornmeal. They looked thin, tired, and sad.

Mr. Stroud took the empty bowls. "Now get going," he ordered.

The three began walking toward the rice fields. Tilly put on her hat and followed them. She crept silently, staying well behind them.

Other slaves were heading out to the fields. Tilly fell in step at the back of the group. She pulled her big hat down over her eyes to hide her face.

When the fieldwork began, Tilly hid in a grove of trees. She stayed there all morning. Her eyes never left her parents. Side by side, they worked under the sun. Mr. Stroud watched them closely.

When Tilly grew thirsty, a nearby stream offered a cool drink. Her stomach growled, but Tilly didn't take any food from the bag.

Hour after hour dragged by. Late in the afternoon, a chestnut mare trotted toward the field. Mr. Stroud turned to see who was riding up.

Tilly dashed out of the trees and joined the workers. She moved toward her mother and father. Staying near them, she pretended to pull weeds.

"Whoa," Lydia ordered the chestnut mare. Then she called out to Mr. Stroud.

"What is it, Miss Lydia?" he asked.

"My horse seems to be limping," Lydia said. "She might have a stone in her shoe. Come take a look."

"Yes, Miss Lydia." Mr. Stroud went to help Lydia.

Tilly scurried up between her parents. "It's Tilly!" she hissed to them. "Don't make a sound. Just follow me. Hurry."

The field had been flooded a short time ago. With each step, their feet sank into deep mud. Once they reached the trees, they began to run.

Lydia was speaking loudly to Mr. Stroud. Her voice had to cover the sound of their flight. As if to help, the other slaves began to sing.

Tilly dared not look back. Lydia would keep Mr. Stroud busy as long as she could. But what if the plan hadn't worked? What if Mr. Stroud had seen them go?

On and on they fled. They splashed across the stream. The underbrush became thicker. Now they were better hidden. Still they had to keep going.

"Tilly!" Kwaku called out at last.

Tilly stopped. Had something gone wrong? She turned to see Catbird leaning against a tree.

"Your mother needs to rest," Kwaku said.

"And we both need to hug you," Catbird panted.

Tilly didn't know which parent to embrace first. Kwaku was closest to her. She threw her arms around him. Then she flew to her mother. Catbird wept as she held Tilly close.

They sat in the shade to rest. Tilly opened the bag. They each ate a piece of fruit.

Tilly had so much to tell her parents. But talking was not safe. People would be searching the woods, listening for them.

At last Kwaku spoke. "We must keep moving," he said softly.

The three got up and walked on. Suddenly Catbird grabbed Kwaku's arm. "Do you hear something?" she asked.

They stopped to listen. Tilly gasped. She heard men's voices and barking dogs.

"Keep going," Kwaku said. "But be as quiet as you can. Maybe we'll find a stream. If we walk in water, the dogs will lose our scent."

They had to go slowly. Running made too much noise. The men and dogs were catching up.

"I don't see any water," Catbird whispered.

"We'd better get out of sight," Kwaku said. "We'll hide deep in the bushes."

They burrowed in among leaves and branches. Twigs scratched Tilly's face and arms. Her heart pumped wildly.

The footsteps and voices were now just yards away. The dogs began to yelp and whine.

"They must be nearby!" a voice shouted. It was Mr. Miller.

"Should we let the dogs loose?" Mr. Stroud asked.

Tilly was sure she'd pass out. Everything she did went wrong. Now she and her parents would be attacked by the dogs. Later they'd have to face severe punishment by Mr. Stroud.

Then she heard another sound. A horse was galloping up. Lydia's voice rang out. "Father, wait!"

"Lydia!" Mr. Miller exclaimed. "What are you doing here?"

"I think I saw them," Lydia said. "I rode as fast as I could to tell you."

"Where did you see them?" Mr. Miller asked.

"A few miles away in the other direction," Lydia lied.

"But what about the dogs?" Mr. Stroud asked. "Something has them all excited."

"They probably smell a wild animal," Lydia said.

"Are you certain you saw them?" Mr. Miller asked.

"I saw what looked like three slaves running," Lydia said. "But they were far north of here."

"We'd better turn back," Mr. Miller said.

"But, sir—" Mr. Stroud began.

Tilly, Kwaku, and Catbird held their breath.

"My valuable property is getting away," Mr. Miller barked. "I have no time to waste on a raccoon hunt. We'll follow Lydia."

The frantic dogs were pulled away. The men moved off through the woods. Silence fell. Tilly and her parents didn't move for a long time.

"I think it's safe now," Catbird said at last.

They wriggled out into the open. Tilly still clutched the bag of food.

At first they walked without saying a word. Then Catbird asked, "Who do you think Lydia saw?"

"She didn't see anyone," Tilly said. "She lied to save us."

"Why on earth would she do that?" Kwaku asked.

"It was part of the plan," Tilly answered.

"What plan?" Catbird wanted to know.

Tilly grinned and joined hands with her parents. She told the story as they walked along.

"You were very brave," Kwaku said when Tilly finished.

"You've made us both proud," Catbird added.

Later they stopped by a creek for supper. They shared a loaf of bread and drank from the stream.

The weary family lay down at dusk. Tilly fell asleep as soon as she closed her eyes.

🌿 🌿 🌿

Breakfast was a piece of fruit for each person. More water helped to fill them up.

"Where will we go now, Father?" Tilly asked.

"I heard talk in the fields," Kwaku said. "Chief Bowlegs and the black Seminoles have started new towns. I know where to look for them."

"Is it far?" Tilly asked.

"Yes," Kwaku told her. "The new towns are 120 miles south of the old ones."

"I don't mind," Tilly said. "It will be worth every step."

They rose to continue on their way. They hadn't gone far when they heard something.

"It sounds like a horse," Catbird whispered.

"Oh, no," Tilly groaned. "Not again."

Once more they took cover in the brush.

"I hear something else," Kwaku said.

Someone was singing. Tilly recognized the song and the woman's voice.

"It's Samantha!" Tilly exclaimed.

She parted the branches. Sure enough, along came Samantha astride the chestnut mare. Samson rode behind her.

Tilly scrambled out of the bushes. Kwaku and Catbird followed.

"How did you find us?" Tilly cried.

"Miss Lydia told us which way you were going," Samson explained. "She sent her father and Mr. Stroud on a wild-goose chase. Then she came to our cabin."

"She told us everything," Samantha continued. "And she sent us after you. She wanted us to bring this to Tilly."

Samantha held out a flat brown package. Tilly took the parcel. She already knew what was inside.

Tilly didn't know all the words. But she knew ways to figure them out. She would keep working at it. One day she would read the book from cover to cover.

Kwaku wasn't pleased. "What a terrible thing," he said. "You rode so far through the woods. And all because of a spoiled child."

Samantha and Samson looked at each other. They began to chuckle.

Samson got down from the horse. Then he helped his wife dismount. He turned the horse toward the Miller Plantation.

"Giddyap," Samson said. He slapped the horse's rump. The animal trotted back through the woods.

"Why did you do that?" Catbird asked. "How will you get home?"

"By walking with you," Samson answered.

"Tilly wants us to meet some friends of hers," Samantha explained.

Samson winked at Tilly. "One is named Tiger," he said. "Another is called Abraham."

"Well, I'll be," Kwaku said. Then he laughed aloud and clapped Samson on the back.

"We'll never get there by standing around," Tilly said. "Let's go."

Linking arms, the five began their long journey.

Timeline

February 12, 1813   White settlers from Georgia and Tennessee rode into Florida. They destroyed Bowlegs Town and the maroon town nearby. These towns were later rebuilt on the Suwannee River.

July 27, 1816   Fort Mosa was destroyed at Andrew Jackson's order.

January 1817   Alexander Arbuthnot arrived in Florida. He soon opened a trading post on the Suwannee River near the Seminoles.

June 17, 1817   Seminole leaders named Arbuthnot their agent. He wrote letters for them to the governments of Britain, Spain, and the United States.

December 1817–   Indians and white settlers
Spring 1818   near the Florida-Georgia border fought off and on.

March 9, 1818	Andrew Jackson learned that escaped slaves were at the Spanish fort at St. Marks. Seminoles and Arbuthnot were there too. Jackson decided to march against St. Marks. Then he would continue east.
April 2, 1818	Arbuthnot sent a letter of warning to the Suwannee River Trading Post.
April 6, 1818	Andrew Jackson captured St. Marks and put Arbuthnot in prison.
April 8, 1818	Jackson and 3,500 men marched toward Bowlegs Town and Nero's Town. The towns were 107 miles east of St. Marks. Arbuthnot's warning reached the Suwannee River Trading Post.

April 16, 1818, *3:00 p.m.*	Six Seminole scouts saw Jackson's troops six miles away. Chief Bowlegs had already taken his villagers into the swamp to hide. Some Indian Seminole warriors stayed to join in the fighting. The scouts rode to warn Nero's people. Black families were still ferrying across the Suwannee to safety. Jackson's army arrived at sunset, and the battle began.
April 28, 1818	Creek scouts, searching six miles beyond the river, captured five black Seminoles and nine Indian Seminole women and children.
May 24, 1818	Jackson took Pensacola from Spain.

August 1818	President Monroe returned St. Marks and Pensacola to Spain. The United States government had not approved Jackson's invasion of Florida.
1826	Abraham had become an important black Seminole chief. He was known as the Prophet Abraham.